Trio

Toni Mirosevich
Charlotte Muse
Edward Smallfield

2/5/95

Alice,
It's been a great gift + priviledge
for me to know you + to read your
work. These poems have benefited
enormously from your sensitivity
as a critic + from your example as
a writer — your courage, your

Specter Press: Albany, California

dedication, + your talent. You've
a brilliant writer, — I've learned
so much from you, + your encouragement
and support have critical in my
growth as a poet.

Love,
Ed

The three poets wish to acknowledge
the contributions of Frances Mayes
to the making of this book:
her rigorous and generous attention;
her encouragement and support.

© 1995 Toni Mirosevich, Charlotte Muse, Edward Smallfield
Library of Congress Catalog Card Number: 94-12045
ISBN 0-9645026-0-7

Cover design by Cathy McAuliffe
Cover photograph by Anita Schriver

Specter Press
1009 Peralta Avenue
Albany, CA 94706

Acknowledgements

Alchemy: How to Swallow a Frog

Americas Review: Until Winds Can Blow This Wind Away, Where Memory Is Stored

The Best of Fresh Hot Bread II: Flies

Bottomfish: Labor Day

Caliban: Blood, Self-Portrait with Thorn Necklace and Hummingbirds, Sleepless Nights, Stain

Ink: Doll Boxes, In the Dream of the Tiger, Where Memory Is Stored

Magazine: Pink Harvest

Manoa: How the Late October Novel Begins, Prostate, Secret Lives

Margin: Insomnia

Painted Hills Review: Black Dog, February 14, 1994, Firenze, Running

Poetry Flash: Where Memory Is Stored

The San Francisco Bay Guardian: Limited Versions

The Seattle Review: Tools of the Trade

SFSU Review: August, Improvisation

Through the Mill: Labor Day

Transfer: Doll Boxes, Flies, Home Movie, How to Swallow a Frog, In the Dream of the Tiger, Night Light through a Pleated Shade, Smelt, Tilting, Tools of the Trade, Veering, We Must Learn to Seem Empty

Visions International: Song Line through my House

Zapisdat World Anthology: A Poet at the End of the World, The Sun Muffled, the Pond Crowded, Turning to Stone

ZYZZYVA: Bread and Butter Note, Cattaraugus Creek

Contents

Toni Mirosevich

Charlotte Muse

Edward Smallfield

Toni Mirosevich

Tools of the Trade

I turn my back as he unbuttons his shirt, the fifth article
taken off (first, a heavy coat brought from the old country,
under that a new one—light, flimsy—given at the point of entry,
then a discarded suitjacket, a cardigan, now the flannel shirt).

His fingers, no longer supple, labor down the buttons. Sent
to cobalt mines, he worked the Ukraine thirty years, hands
curved round a pick and hammer. He tells this to the interpreter
who in turn tells me. Something is lost. I imagine caves full of
dark blue stone, blue glass that shatters with every hammer
brought down.

They all come in with stories: Zena, with her tired bones,
Nadeshda with her cough. Exposed to cobalt, to the regime, he
places his body before me, offers it up. Given everything: How
did this man survive? With the tools of my trade, a faith in the
tangible, I search for clues (a strong constitution? a vigorous
heart?), hold the stethoscope in my hands to warm it, to give
his body one less shock.

When I turn and lift the gown—hospital regulation, small
blue stars across thin white cloth, a picture of the heavens—I
find his body covered with faint blue lines, as if the gown were
never raised. Looking closer, angels kneel on either side of his
chest, face each other, hands clasped over the heart. As he
breathes the wings on their backs expand, flutter.

He tells the interpreter the angels were tattooed on long ago,
to protect him from Stalin. His life has been lifted on their
wings. What lesser mystery could have guaranteed his passage
to this exam room, my care, to the soft rubber hammer at his
knees?

Smelt

He is off somewhere with other fishermen on the dock.
Bullshitting about the season, quotas, about Alaska.
I collect pieces of twine, stray bits left over
where men were mending the nets. Earlier I watched
as they sewed the holes a dolphin or shark had torn.

I tie the pieces together in a long line, the way
convicts tie sheets together to lower their bodies
down, and then hook a safety pin on the end with
a torn piece of bologna found in the galley, the meat
already beginning to turn gray around the edges.
The fish won't know the difference.

In my dreams fish are pulled up hand over fist.
I haul them in, their silver bodies with a hint of
twitch, a satisfied look on their faces, this last
bite of sandwich a last supper. The fish always
take what I offer, satisfied with the gift.

Over the edge, too near the edge (where is the hand
to stop me, where is the warning voice) I drop the
line, watch the pin pierce the water and wait. I
lift the hook out again and again. The bait comes
up unaltered, no tear, no telling mark. When he
returns I have nothing to show. We climb into
the Jeep, the sun cutting out a section of sky
like a round hole in the netting for us to
escape through.

Once he and I went out at night, just the two of us.
With hooks placed at intervals on the wire, every
inch or so, we watched glints of metal disappear
into the black water below. Soon the poles began
to hum. In the moonlight the smelt came up like
Christmas bells on the line of hooks, each bell
attached and ringing.

Tilting

Stilnovich came down the alley, bowlegged as if a cannon had shot through, hair parted and combed, wearing someone's discarded suitjacket, past its prime, as was Stilnovich.

When he came to where the alley dead-ended into a backyard he stopped, found the arbor, crossed the threshold into the garden (perhaps not the only threshold crossed that day, maybe soon the bride swung up like a feather or a sack of potatoes, the door kicked in, the promise of a new life).

Zorka was digging in the azaleas, pouring fish fertilizer on the plants, overpowering any sweet scent of garden—the gladiolas by the fence, the honeysuckle, the plum tree in bloom—all this no match for fish, dead and ground, a thick brown liquid that would revive the unconscious and then knock them dead again.

She looked up, saw him there, tilting in the breeze, fumbling with his jacket buttons, up to something. What did he want this time? The accordion? A jug of wine?

He spoke first. "How are you, Mrs. Dragovich?" He used the formal greeting out of respect for her husband who had long since passed on, who had died at sea. "What are you doing this fine morning?"

"Scratching myself," she said under her breath. What does it look like, fool.

"What's that?"

"A little of this, a little of that."

There was a long silence. She poured fertilizer with a new vengeance. He continued to tilt in the wind, his face full of spring, as if his nose were stuffed with roses.

There was a rustling, leaves or the scrape of grapevines on the trellis. He cleared his throat.

"I don't mean to change the subject but, will you marry me?"

The breeze died down, and with the question, as if slapped, she revived, her sense of smell suddenly keen, as if she could smell the man who had inhabited the suitjacket before Stilnovich, could remember the way her husband's scent lay on the pillow in the mornings, a mix of cigar and fish and the sea.

She stopped, weighing the proposition.

"What you got?" she asked.

"I got a house."

"I got a house too."

He tilted his hat and turned to go. Bending back over a plant she heard a quick snap, looked up in time to see him pluck a pink camellia blossom off the bush, fit it into his lapel. As he moved away she was standing on the dock, eyes to the horizon, watching her husband's boat fade in the distance, as she now watched Stilnovich get smaller, his walk down the alley to his house, no hesitation, sure of step. Without warning he changed course. Turning into Mrs. Vitalich's garden, he passed under a new arbor—palms open, hopeful, ready to receive.

Until Winds Can Blow This Wind Away

1

The sky changes but doesn't change.
Clouds outside her window are like
clouds she saw an hour ago, cumulus shapes
the children named: rocking horse, flying fish.
When she raises her chin, breathes deep,
there is no smell. The only sound sirens
from the plant, long, continuous.

In the village of Chernobyl all routine stops.

Last week this was just a dirt road,
this the gate, off its hinge, to the garden,
and here, the short cut through the field.
There was no greater significance
to the landscape. The children
came home early from school, a holiday
out of the blue. At the fencepost
the spotted dog wagged its feathered tail.

2

Not long after government men come
with funeral money. Five children,
five allotments. One can't predict
what might fall, what might blanket them
in their beds. Standing in the doorway,
she holds her baby, the smallest, shields
his face from the morning sun, then asks
"are there signs," to no reply.
After they leave she puts the rubles
in the blue jar with the tight lid.
As if these too might crumble.

At night she awakens her husband with a dream.
Under the floorboards, under the sod
he will dig deep holes,
put the children there, protected,
the way she planted seeds last spring
in dark soil. The cabbage grew large
as faces, the beets a field of dark red hearts.
She will plant the children
until the sky changes,
until winds can blow this wind away.

3

In the new city the ground is gray,
cemented over. Here there is less soil.
At the playground her children
climb a jungle gym,
then lay themselves down on the asphalt
to draw pictures with colored chalk:
a sun with arrowed rays, a spotted dog.
The clouds above move swiftly.
A wind starts up. Their reddened cheeks
bloom over stiff new parkas.
As she watches she repeats the incantation:
they are healthy, they are healthy
then sees something dark and turns her eyes away.

That night she asks her husband:
is this the reason why—the shy one, her favorite—
is this the first sign,
how the boy now uses his left hand
and not his right?

Veering

I got started thinking about characterization. A student asked me—the new writing teacher—for some tips on how to flesh out a character and I gave her a list of questions to ask. But in real life how do you respond to the question: height, weight, age? If a mugger succeeds in grabbing your purse and you get a quick glimpse before being knocked to the pavement, how *do* you tell age? This has particular relevance. Just last week I was walking in the Marina on one of those terrifically cold days we sometimes get, the wind full of gusts, white caps on the bay, a few hardy souls out "braving it," you had to lean into your step. I was on the home stretch, coming back from having walked out to Ft. Point, on that cinder path parallel to Crissey Field when I saw a man coming toward me, well, not towards me, let's say he was headed in my direction. He was weaving a bit, he did not look purposeful, he was "braving" nothing, acting as if it was 70 degrees, the kind of weather that causes one to amble. It was this that caught my eye at first, his amble, not the fact that there seemed to be a spot on the front of his pants, where the legs meet is the delicate way to put it, a spot a bit oddly placed. I thought of rock stars who sew some decal—a bursting sun, an STP sticker—on their jeans right over their privates to catch the eye, as if this were necessary, their jeans already a second skin, so tight you could see the outline of a dime in their back pocket, could tell if the coin were heads or tails. As we drew closer I noticed this decal wasn't a spot, there was some movement and as objects became more distinct, form became subject—identify the concrete thing I would tell my class—I realized it was his penis, he was a flasher without any of the obvious accoutrements of his profession, no Army coat thrown open to unveil at the last moment his little prize like a piece of art for the National Museum, no official leer, that "I've Got a Secret" look. There appeared to be no desire to cover or expose, no flair, just his penis bob bob bobbing along, and the first thing I thought was, my god, it's so damn cold out, what kind of fool would be walking with a delicate body part exposed, get a down comforter on that thing.

But there were second thoughts and third, I realized my thoughts were speeding up as we neared each other on the path,

I was scared now, wondering *rapidly* what kind of person would be walking out on the promenade with johnny jump up outside of his pants and to what purpose. I did the right thing, tried to avert my eyes but noticed in my peripheral vision that he was veering, he was veering off course—getting off the subject I might tell my class—listing to the right, like the boats on the bay, coming towards me, it was the veering that upset me, it was him coming into my path and at ten feet (when does a veer become a lunge?) I took off, I began to run, no longer interested in contemplating whether or not he was cold, whether or not he was ambling. The odd thing is he broke into a run too, in the opposite direction, almost as if we both had started a race at the same time, the gun having gone off and it was first one to the finish line, some doppelgänger motif written into a student's story—my "exposed" double running away from the other self.

I thought of the woman behind me, an older woman I had passed on the path, who certainly wouldn't be as fleet of foot and I went to the nearest building, 100 yards away, some military outpost and asked to use the phone, called the Presidio police, got a nice official fellow on the line, his calming voice, his ability to cut through peripheral matter, to stay on the subject, and one of the first questions he asked was: what would you say was the man's age?

I couldn't say, I didn't know—20's, 30's, 40's? Was he a youthful forty or an aging twenty, worn down from such constant contact with the elements? I thought of his penis, how *does* one tell penis age, it looked relatively youthful, but then I didn't see the rest of the apparatus which might have lent a clue, how things stretch, lose elasticity, the effects of time. I hesitated, I resisted giving my opinion, was age all that important, weren't there other identifying factors (the sweatshirt, his frayed jeans)—use specific detail, concrete detail, the best way to flesh out character I tell my class—and weren't we missing some essential point of the story, that being: could a person be arrested for veering?

Improvisation

Here she is not afraid. Of the neighbor with a glass turned over and placed against the wall, a small strain of jazz overheard. Enough proof to call the authorities. (Definition of authorities in Russia: anyone other than you.) Imagine it. Louis Armstrong as ticket to the hoosegow. If feet tap to the music, feet tramp down the hall.

(Her father, who is unhappy here, calls everyday. When talking of home he says the same phrase over and over again: "I was always afraid *and* I was happy.")

"We always whispered," she yells over the Coltrane I have on to make her feel at ease. Between cuts a quick silence opens. She brings her voice down low, draws her lips in tight, small. Still wary. "Do you know anyone who would want to go back? Anyone?"

I put on Brubeck. She tells me how music was smuggled in, the risk taken. Sailors, in from the Black Sea, slipped tapes from pocket to pocket, this while the crew unloaded cargo (each move closely watched, each box counted once, twice.) Late at night, somewhere in Odessa, they would find a lab. With X-ray film, a grooving needle, an amplifier, somehow a rough copy was made. The scratchy horn of Miles on "Kind of Blue," Ella's scat. The world of improvisation. Deviation from the score.

When she's finished the tale I say "Where there's a will..." some platitude, a way to buy time. Only to have this surface later: Why did we believe that it was different with them—not in their fiber to resist, to improvise? As if the glum faces seen on the nightly news were unable, unwilling to carry a tune?

Before the evening's over we go through all of *Take Five,* all of *A Love Supreme.* Each time I reach for the volume knob she laughs. I crank it up and up and up till the floor shakes. The neighbor next door pounds back with her broom handle, a one two beat, perfect syncopation.

When she leaves I go straight to bed, pull the cover up over my head to keep the chill away. What will I ever have to compare, what can come close? Nothing in my world provides a translation. Then, in the next beat, one slim memory surfaces like a stray riff: nights spend under cover, my mother's soft foot fall by the door, a small pink transistor held to the ear, the precious precious sound.

Bread and Butter Note

The small things apply. A note for the book. Some response to say it meant a lot, you noticed the effort, you're still with the world.

So you select a card from the pile you keep in a drawer—the first decision: blank or printed, the over-used Hoppers or the opium flowers or the Frankenthaler card you've been saving for someone special—and you place in a note, a thank you, something penned as if off the cuff, with airy jottings but each small word counted, weighed all the way to *yours truly* or *with affection* or the wide distanced *sincerely*, the name signed once, then thrown out, how the end letter dipped too low, indicated something not right (you don't want to weigh her down). Another penned, the right lilt this time, then stamped, then sealed, all of that activity, odd what has become effort.

Carrying it from desk to the telephone stand beside the door, placing it there, you imagine its journey, hearing that just this morning they arrested a postal worker who had squirreled away thousands of letters in his apartment because he was exhausted, couldn't keep up with the work. You think of bags of letters filling his room, no room to breathe, then remember the story of the woman with millions of cats in her small studio, all of them pressing in on her, all the crying voices, so many that she had a bed constructed in the center of the room covered in chicken wire, the one place she had to get away.

Looking at the letter again, something's wrong, it's incomplete, a wide plain of white where the street address should be. You think it's Pine or Spruce or maybe a deciduous tree, you can't be certain, you're less sure of so many things, so you search for the address book, something you haven't picked up in days. Once in hand there's that cavalcade of names, all those letters, a and b and C, whom you never called, she sick with cancer and you not calling, the last time you saw her she was wizened away and if you don't call soon there will be less of her, less of her, fewer pills in the bottle, another reminder that the gamma globulin bottle is low, *your* potion number 9, what you shoot in to give you energy. Funny how it doesn't seem to be doing its job, the stuff in you but you cannot track it, deposited in some dead letter office, otherwise the book wouldn't feel so heavy in your hand, the weight of it, all the calls you haven't made. You quick find the right name, the right street but not before lifting the phone, who can lift you, cordless you must wait, the small indecision before the dial tone, then hang up when the machine comes on. It is like this, don't you see, each measured movement and what will it cost, each page calls, first a trio, then a quartet, and then the community chorus, all the crying voices, and the only thing that saves you, the one thing you have done, is to put the address down, it's ready to go, the small things apply, you have sent your bread and butter note.

Where Memory Is Stored

They lined them up, the Khmer Rouge liking order, people lay
on the ground and soldiers came and hacked off their heads,
heads full of disorder. Heads rolled, large and small, given
their roundness. He too felt the blade but somehow—though his
neck was half severed—his head did not roll.

*You remember certain things, forget others. Did the birds as
witness stop singing? Did the trees stand still? Did soldiers,
exhausted from the task, stop and rest? Was it tiring work,
lopping off heads and stacking them up like round stones piled
high to make a wall?*

That night, he disappears into the jungle. As he runs, he
wonders: Why chop off the heads and not the feet?

When the head is severed memory spills onto the ground, into
the river. The Mekong is muddy—not with silt, not with runoff
from monsoons but with memory. The ground is so drenched
your toes squish in the wet wet soil. The Khmer Rouge are
smart. They know the ground will dry, know in time the river
will run clear. There will be no record except for bones stacked
in a wall, like a mosaic, in a certain order, the Khmer Rouge
liking order. In time, the skulls, scrubbed clean by the sun,
hollow like whistles, seem to make a sound.

*If you took one of the skulls in your hands, once someone's
relation, someone you knew, you could blow into the eyes, like
when you blow into the top of a bottle and get some sound but it
would be nonspecific. It might seem like a moan if you were
listening for a moan. Or how your aunt let air out through the
space between her teeth in a low whistle. But it's just a hollow
sound, your breath in a round cavern—it is not the person's
scream. In the same way, you could make up memory, place it*

there but it wouldn't be the same as the memory that came before, that spilled out.

The man runs in the jungle for a long time. Then he is in a camp. Then he is on a plane.

In America he hears, "Oh these refugees they've come to steal our jobs." This is what people say who somehow forget that they supported Pol Pot, they forget.

When he sees a man in uniform (a Pinkerton guard, the man in the elevator) he stands still, he does not move. When his brother-in-law is beating his wife he doesn't call the police, remembering it is better to have a screaming wife than a wife with no head. At night he dreams of rivers overrunning their banks, on an entire country submerged.

Thinking back you might imagine you hear laughter or crying in the trees but it is all your imagination. It is what you place there.

Pink Harvest

She stands at the kitchen window, fillets the salmon, slices a straight line down the belly of the fish. She could do this in her sleep. Outside the window the sky is full of red clouds, the kind that appear only in winter. Red sky in the morning, sailor take warning. Red sky at night, sailor's delight. Since it's afternoon she breathes a sigh of relief.

The front door opens. He comes in, plants a kiss, longer than usual, then throws a fat package on the drainboard. She picks up the package to weigh it, her hands accurate scales, figures she's dealing with three pounds of something. Without further ceremony tosses off the newsprint. Inside a mound of pure pink fans out, the color so vivid it takes a moment for her eyes to adjust. She looks closer. The shrimp become distinct, individual. Some lie hooked together, entwined, a baby's finger curled around the mother's. Take a good look, he says. Pink harvest of the sea.

He starts in, tries to sell her on a new gamble. As if her whole life with him isn't one. Someone has gotten hold of his ear, convinced him of money to be earned fishing shrimp instead of salmon, the salmon he has spent a lifetime tracking. He reaches down, scoops some up, the shrimp dripping through his fingers. He believes in the possibility of a big return, can picture his hands plowing through piles of money, green bills floating through the air. She notices how small the shrimp are. So pink. So feminine. How they drift down like petals. How can he risk their economic future on something so delicate?

He asks her to look at this a different way. He tells her to let her eyes drift, adjust her sights downwards. He tells her the bottom of the sea is pink.

He will illustrate his point. Outside the kitchen window the sky is red. The sea will be calm tomorrow, something she knows to be true. He builds on that, predicts a glowing future, says the sky is a reflection—not of the sunset—but of what lies below the waves.

There is no hindsight at the start of a journey, no indication of outcome. All we have is what we can conjure. She turns back to the cutting board, tries to think: how the color of the sky can influence the water, how the bottom of the ocean can influence the sky.

Silent Witness

I'm outside on the back deck, driven from the front of the house where I usually work, where my desk sits. Above the desk is a picture window, bird's eye view of the world, the new kid who's moved into the foster care house kitty-corner to mine, a tough guy, small time hood. There's something about him though, a magnetism. Now gangs convene, fight it out on his lawn, sport colors and stances and hand signals that distract.

Out here in back there's a view of Milagra Ridge, protected open space, empty except for a white van, a crew of California Conservation Corps teens, up there weeding out non-indigenous plants so native plants can grow, digging up ice plant, oxalis, a botanic cleansing as it were. Last week they took down the few remaining cypress trees and chopped the trunks into pieces, small enough to be carted home for the cold cold nights to come.

It's been heating up for some time, this war zone outside my picture window, and after the incident with the ice pick Sunday, one kid scratching a skull and bones into the hood of the new kid's car, a friend said I should call the Silent Witness Program for some intervention, that's what they're there for. It's not my nature to banter with the boys in blue but I figure if things continue I'll give it a shot.

When I woke up this morning I had wanted to write something nice, something poetic, but I couldn't get a bead on a poem, couldn't concentrate with the action across the street, watching kids tote soft luggage bags out of the foster house, packing something (a pistol? a luger?) and then pile into the car, ready for a joy ride. When they took off the car backfired, sound of snipers,

and I ended up writing something down about Yugoslavia, how we're all witness to that hell, can watch from our safe window on the world as villagers cut down the few remaining trees in Sarajevo for fuel, the town square now free of foliage. I found myself longing for the past, a world without ethnic cleansing, for Tito, his magnetism, someone people could believe in, who could put the country back together again.

The neighborhood's got a bad egg, that's how I see it, this boy
who's practicing for the big time. We hear him croon, fucking
this, fucking that, Johnny one note, a small Sinatra, but like Frank
he's charismatic, a bully with charm, can bring the gang together.
I see them out there in their knit caps and baggy pants, Dean
Martin and Sammy Davis, and Peter Lawford, Robin and The
Seven Hoods. They visit at set intervals, *Night and Day*,

and it took a friend to say drugs before I even got it. I'd rather
keep mum, isn't that what poets do, take down images, the view of
the hills, the dew, the light, silent witness to the morning, hard
work but not as hard as the CCC are working, sun glinting off the
orange vests someone makes them wear so they won't get lost in
the brush up there weeding out the bad elements,

which is what I'd like to do to the kid who's taking over, not of
this neighborhood, not indigenous. He's not like the block
regulars, reggae man and the graffiti artist and the big Russian kid
who plays hookey to take his mother to the clinic every
Wednesday, and now, in the middle of this, a shot goes off, a
quick pop from the street and this is all it takes.

I dial up the number. A woman gets on the line and when I ask her
name she can't tell me, see she's anonymous too, "we're all silent
witnesses," she says and maybe there's the truth. I give her license
numbers and when she asks if I've heard any monikers—how they
track gang members nowadays—the first thing I can think of to tell
her is *Old Blue Eyes is back*.

By the time we finish talking all the kids have driven off, their
work done, the CCC kids in their white van, the gang in the hot
car. I don't want to intervene, just want them out of my view so I
can write something elegant and spare and pastoral, a poem with
clear images, colors: the orange vests, navy of the knit caps, green
of the uniforms as troops shell the city, an exact match for the
once green Milagra hills.

Limited Versions

We get the story second hand.

1.

He worked in a stationery store in Viet Nam. Hard for us here, in this country, to imagine people penning letters during the war, to imagine the act of writing or correspondence, normal activities in a day,

the limited version on the nightly news.

2.

He met his wife through the mail. They were pen pals, she in the North, he in the South, part of a cultural exchange to promote understanding. He felt she understood him. She, in turn, felt drawn to him: the soft scent of his letters.

This is how they fell in love.

3.

They met and married. Had a garden. Had a son. On her off hours she helped in the stationery store, a better head for business. On his off hours he studied painting, quick brush strokes to show flowers from his garden as they came into bloom.

A way to secure a record.

4.

When Saigon fell they fled on a boat, they hurried, but not in the way you or I know, normal activities in a day, a time line to meet, the dry cleaners, the kids to practice, hurry meaning life or death.

(another piece of the story: the child would die at sea.)

5.

All is past. In this country he finds a job, an interpreter in a refugee health clinic. After listening to people tell their stories to the doctor, after people tell his story again and again, he

must hurry, the paper on the exam table his palette. Where their
lives have been examined, where his life has been examined, he
draws blooms,

roses, peonies, the orange red burst of flames.

6.
Meanwhile his wife has learned real estate. She wants to wheel
and deal and forget. They argue. She tells him paper is perishable.
Not like rock or brick or stone. With savings she buys house after
rundown house. If one falls there will always be another standing
somewhere.

Who knows what she has seen?

7.
A nurse sees his work, buys a painting. He does not tell his wife.
With the money he makes he sends home for two chops, the red
signature stamp at the edge of the canvas. One chop his name, the
other a saying he puts on every print:

"beauty makes for a longer life."

8.
We get the story third hand. In the paper, limited versions. There's
talk of immigrants, refugees, there's talk of jobs. Here's the gist of
it: They will take from us, they will take from us.

(What was taken from them? What was taken from her?)

9.
His drawings are taped up like the pictures of children to exam
room walls, to remind the staff, given their limited version of
history, of what they cannot imagine, to remind him when he
walks in and sees them

he had a garden there.

Where You Go for Comfort

1

Late at night inside your room:

> not into the past, to hearth, mother, night light in the
> hall, no doting one, a grandma, kitchen lamp and
> something from the oven, the art of care, or quiet
> strength, what men were, the arms of the fireman who
> lifted you, age 5, and took you from your burning house,
> your crib, and Augie Doggie going up in smoke.

> nor into the present, a cozy room, books, friends
> gathered round, willing to tell you all you are is good.
> The one you love would try to fix things, distract. She
> doesn't know where you go when you are like this. (You
> remember a passage from something. *"He would cast
> about in his mind for some words that might console her,
> and would find only lame and useless ones."*)

2

Seated at your desk, you take the book down, a life ring, and read:

> *"...his own identity was fading out into a grey impalpable
> world: the solid world itself which these dead had one time
> reared and lived in was dissolving and dwindling."* You
> forgot it was this easy, this safe, to slip away and every time
> you tried to ask for help, the effort caught you. The computer
> screen lies black before you, the black blank screen, slashes
> of white where once the cursive rolled and rolled. You read
> on *"...softly falling into the dark mutinous Shannon
> waves..."* and this is close, the entry. You ride it out, this
> image, until you're on the sea.

The crew sleeps below. The captain is gone. You take the
helm, like your father taught you. The fathommeter's broken (what
folly to think we'd ever know depth) though for a moment soft

green light comes from the dial, the first invitation, sea green. The ship to shore is on but useless. Where there was life now there's only static, some last attempt to tell them that you loved them but then again that never worked.

Here nothing ties. You're out there, in the center of the ocean, the sky black, sea black and now the only light may be from a star, a night light in the hall. The waves crash and peak, the sea is roiling, that's what people say back home where words are important and weighed.

Everything is fictional, your life to this point. One look at the waves and you go under, this is what you came for, but you needn't worry. There is no boat, no structure. You haven't a body now so there's no turmoil in the roiling, rolling waves. You slip in, where you go for comfort, here in this study, your dark room on the sea.

quotes from "The Dead" by James Joyce

Charlotte Muse

Why You're Afraid of the Road

There is room for one car, but what if the wheels
miss and the car hangs over the edge
with two tires spinning? You'd be moving frantically
against the door, hoping to keep the balance
or get out. Never would the yellow dust of the road seem
so desirable; the blue sky so thin and threatening—
and you a turned-over turtle, a blind bird.

Or what if you just drove off the edge
because you were tired of all
curves and wanted to lie on air?

Whether or not spirits come back,
empty and blue and unable to hold anything,
you could say you'd gone into their place
in your body. Of course
you love life;
it holds you as hard as death does.
Everything holds you but the air
and this is why you're afraid of the road.

Dream House

Twilight has come to the street of comfortable houses,
which slopes down to a darkness, then ends.
Is there a river at the bottom? An orchard?
There's no gleam on fruit or on water.

In the windows of the brown Dutch colonial
electric candles shine. Behind them
closed shutters, and darkness yawning into rooms.
These rooms slope away from the light.

The house is dark, or only the upper rooms, dark;
downstairs a party's about to begin. The parents
have tiptoed away. Their children stare from their beds
as the billion dots of darkness gather.

Light is going out of the house. Its candles serve
watch. Nice if their gleam enters the rooms.
Boom! goes the town cannon, signifying night
with its dark plumes gathering.

Boom! go our lives, people think when they hear it;
crashing like water down a flume while
we look for gleam. As darkness approaches,
we fear every shadow.

In the tomb, with no breath to blow darkness away,
we'll break into millions. Yet shadows are formed
from small points of darkness.
See how they gather.

Turning to Stone

Bones go last

After the death bacteria,
hovering close and waiting,
find a way in,
each of the body's cells dies separately

Liquids lose their boundaries;
they drain away.
The smell of rot fades,
the fleshy solids vanish into flattening mounds
furred with grass and melting leaves

But bones lie hard and buried
for centuries
(not dependent, as flesh is, on water for their shape)
and then, at last, begin their crumble

A few bones don't dissolve
They turn to stone

Only one or two
of all the bones in a likely place
makes the transformation.
The reasons are mysterious;
but I believe their power to remake themselves
resembles
feeling

What I've seen of hardening is
refusal
I think somehow
those bones refuse to settle

Every crevice,
every pore and knob
hardens in its place

And then, from wherever
bone-memory is stored
comes change

Home Movie

for Trav and Helen

When my uncle played the old movies he'd salvaged
and turned into videotapes,
there, for an instant,
I was, twenty-five years ago
in the scoop-necked dress I'd worn on a date and then
to my uncle's party the next day,
so I could hold onto a feeling.
My hair swung around my ears and along the curve of my jaw—
shining and sexy! You look like a movie star!
said one of the relatives,
and I was glad the kids were there to hear that.
To see yourself young is like watching
out of the corner of one eye. Something flickers.

You're dead, I said to that girl who was me,
wondering if it was true. My parents are, certainly,
though I could watch their small flat ghosts
walk across the tv and play with the baby.

My uncle lives in the same house he lived in then,
the city is there, though changed,
and there's still the solid feeling of chairs,
the expectation of snow heavy in the pink sky,
the sound of buses ten blocks away just at the edges
of awareness, like cicadas in summer.
Certain birds. The smell of boxwood.

A Poet at the End of the World

Here in the present, where I live, everything
holds still for my naming. I animate whatever I choose.
Do you see the power in this?
Nothing rushes past or pushes forward.
My passions are for the lush body, the green scene.
No abstractions; nothing to die for.

But this time, I want to talk straight to some future
poet and say we know what we're ignoring.
It's not that we don't see it coming—
something has stolen our fire.
I do something and then have delicate feelings about it.

Is this our failure? Did we take our eyes away?
We ask you to understand—it's not because we lack courage.
Connections have broken and each is alone. This is why
we only seem to see ourselves.

You have to watch out.
We've been driven here into this slower *now*—
so many of us saying *I* as loudly as possible.
We're trying to say we matter.
The man on the street—the man lying on the street—
can't say it. We refuse to go so quietly.

We're like the pilgrims who came for a miracle
at Fatima—all standing in the rain under their umbrellas
looking towards the place of a vision.
Some say the sun turned in the sky, or at least shone strangely,
and that everyone who was there saw something.

Musk Ox

Musk ox began as three balls of mud quivering and shivering
to get the particles closer together.
The horns came from something else like fingernails.
That mud kept at it until it got the shape it longed for,
and that's why musk ox will stand out there in terrible cold.
All of them together facing away from the wind.
When you see one,
it's like a giant caterpillar bunched up—
short little legs and one end all face.

Musk Ox Song:
A-home, a-home-home,
A-home, a-hum-hum,
Homola, homola,
(when he runs).

When musk ox walks over the stiff tough willow branches,
he leaves behind clumps of underhair.
So soft, that quiviut! like rainlines.

You see horns curling down, and three brown humps:
one in back of the head, a shoulder hump,
and one before the hind end. A hair skirt.
They tremble in the field glasses, as if in a rear view mirror.
They look like they're moving away.

You'd think you'd have to return
long years back to see musk ox;
he comes out of such large places.
But loons are cackling,
harriers going after smaller birds, the white tail of a ptarmigan
flashing out of the bushes near the owl mound.
Water is pouring over stones, and there he is, there he is.

Flies

The fly father and the uncles are busy
hurling themselves at the window. They swear
in buzz, and refuse to believe
in glass. If they can't see it,
it's not there, that's their story, and meanwhile
the mother is tenderly nestling eggs,
peeled-white and rice-grained,
in the cat food. Always she's rubbing her forelegs
and cocking her head while she considers the six sides
to every question.

To be green-black and filmy-winged,
a nuisance and a plague, germy! To be the carrier
of annoying news, bad news, never good, never good:
no one wants to see flies. To feast on garbage;
to walk on the open eyes of the dead!
To shake oneself into death
buzzing and buzzing while
someone searches for a swatter!

The fly family believes in reincarnation.
When it's your turn to go, they hope
they'll get to take you over,
so next time you'll be spoiler, handwasher,
seeker after decay, swarmer over the world,
unwelcome, fast, persistent.

Night Light through a Pleated Shade

Every night it's the same for me
in the small hours under the comforter.
I turn my head toward the window,
its dim white light,
the faint outlines of the framework
and the darker seams of the shade.

Milky eternal light. The moon too high
to be a circle through the blind.
The room's position
keeps branches from leaving patterns;
there's always even light.

When a neighbor comes home late
his headlights flash
(I've seen them in a dream and know to be afraid)
or sometimes the youngest stands at the bed saying
 "Mommy, I'm scared," in a dream-ridden voice.
These interruptions prove nothing.
The light comes back steady.

It's too gentle to be pitiless
but I know one day I'll go
past the dark dresser and slide away
into that smoothed-out light.

I'm not looking forward to it. I love the oak
and the place where fungus grows wild in rain.
I love my people and my house.
But if I'm alone or in another place
I'll turn my head.
I've practiced dying.

A Farewell

If I ever go back to the place of snows,
and look out of a dark window into white cold,
watching snow fall against a light,
I'll know you will never come to my door.

Looking up as the light flakes
fall out of the dark.
Impossible to see their beginning.
Like the light from the stars

they're coming from the past, where you live now.
If you walked past
my door would be closed and I'd never know
of a line of prints, instantly softening.

But when the sun made shadows of the small craters
your feet left, I'd see the herringbone of a line
going away over the treeless slopes
beyond my yard, something wild.

The Forest

I

I have the picture—
a child's fingerwork, mostly green.
It's a forest with a brownish shape—that's the deer—
in the middleground.

Its majestic head inclines, it offers its profile.
The forefeet splay,
it bends to drink until
in the darkness before moonrise all motion
stops.
The owl freezes on his branch
into a shield or a mask.
The deer turns black, and then,
as the moon's blue-white clears the trees,
turns silver. Leaves are silver;
silver water.

Then sounds,
come soft and homely from the animals,
who must act as if the moon's not there.
A cricket rubs its legs,
a mole plows and piles earth, insects crackle in treebark. A snort
from the deer, a ripple in its coat—movement all around.
The owl's horn sounds.
Everything breathes. Though the deer
is wary, it doesn't run.
At any sudden move it will be gone.

II

In the time when wildness was just around the corner, and wild
strawberries and whippoorwills were out back,
the field was full of fireflies at night
and the blue enamel basin of the tramp and the rags of his clothes
were bundled under the farthest stand of trees.

Into that night field, safe and wild,
went my dreams, to the place where danger and safety were together.

That's how I knew what was in the child's picture.
But the forest went, and the field and garden
while we squandered and fought and gambled and sold—
it's an old story.
Since there's a way in which you can't go
where you haven't been, I'm afraid for the picture.
I thought wild places would stay the same,
with guides to show
what a forest is.
I thought if I went towards safety,
wildness would follow, and if I went towards danger, safety.

I couldn't tell what to defend—
it's an old story. But the wild beauty that was so fragile
took hold in my mind like the strongest weed.
I regret that I didn't stay awake
to watch the horizon on its nightly move closer.
I regret that I never kept watch.
I might have saved the world.

The Sun Muffled, the Pond Crowded

In the dull early winter light,
there must be a thousand birds. Gulls float and shed;
loose feathers drift everywhere.
Coots bob, passive, apparently not even hungry.
Glamorous and temporary Canada geese,
a flock of terns coming in on boomerang wings,
ducks taking off in muscular flight, wild pigeons—
all there, filling up air and water.

Ahead on the path, a man in black with a wide-brimmed hat
appears, walking away into reddish light.
The oily pond surface throws back no reflection,
black shapes fly in low,
the queer light and the crowds of birds don't
change though the man
comes on.

There's a strange suspense,
an increasing alarm of birds, the sun
sullen in spreading cold—
the world unable to bring itself to radiant power.

We think it might react. We wonder if the marshes
that gave up their sweetness to machines
will conspire with the rest of what's destroyed
to strike back. Surely they'll do more
than die.

Along the inlet, an abandoned building with
an old globe of the world visible through a dirty window
sinks into mud left by receding tide.
Though the sun warms through and the sky clears,
innocent and predictable as ever,
we're thinking, half in hope, of earthquakes and drought,
of the man in black.

Love, Arrowhead, Seven, 'V'

The first rock is orange-brown,
with a right-angled smear of white quartz on it:
'L,'   arrowhead,   7,   'V.'
Love,   arrowhead,   seven,   victory.
Love,   this way,   small 'r,'   seven,   wishbone,   bird
flying.

One line of the quartz is wider than the other;
the arrow will pull to the right when it's loosed;
the bird's left wing will shine in the sun.

Love is a victory despite the pain, it flies freely
for awhile (make a wish);
seven is lucky;
so 'r' you.

This way to love; this way means death seven times longer
than we can imagine;
Love is a victory which we believe
we wish for.
Right, is it right?

I used to love as the arrow does.
All my trial was to make a mark
and feel nothing myself.
I thought I was like a bird,
flying above, but the sudden pain!
I could not fly again for seven years.

The other rock is a rain stone;
line after line coming down, coming down,
grey and white, the pink tinge of clouds,
grey, white, all lines coming down, restful,
but we are still holding the stone of harsh orange.
We cannot ignore the writing in the vein of white quartz.
For so long, there has been no rain.
We have tried shooting arrows into the sun

to wound it into love for us,
to cause it to stop watching always.
We have put on bird masks,
so as to be closer;
we have shot seven times,
but the sun is victor.

Now we believe the first rock is a pain stone.
There is no love on it;
'L' and 'r' name directions, only in terms of ourselves.
The victor wishes for power,
the gambler for '7's' and something for nothing.
Our hopes have dwindled to a few questions:
does the arrow point to the other?
can the 'r' mean rain?

How I Came into the Cloth

The cut of the dress was not beautiful, nor was the woman wearing it. Hair frizzed and rusty, upper arms wide and mottled. A bodice with a rounded collar, a turned waistband, a full skirt. When the woman, tired of kneeling erect, or desiring the privacy of her sheltering hands, allowed her back to slump, I could see a sort of pleated effect at the bosom, like a bib.

In the dim light of the church, where the great chandelier is lighted only on feast days, she seemed a plain, pious woman, neither striking nor vibrant. Perhaps she was thrifty; the dress had had a "made" look, a savor of housekeeping magazines and bravely smiling models. But the pattern of the cloth! Where did she find it?

Its background was blue—as rich a blue as will go into glazed cotton. There were shapes that acted as frames for the pattern, and these shapes were flared, like vases, and scrolled around. When I looked into a frame and saw a turret, I came at once to the castle where vine leaves grow about rounded windows, as they grow about the capitals in manuscripts, becoming golden where the monks set shining leaf to the page. No one can keep from using vines—not stonemasons nor woodworkers, weavers nor winemakers—so strong is the sense of life here!

Some of the scrolled frames hold five red-orange roses. These hurt my heart to look at because they are not meant to be close to the life. The flattening of roses is always an ominous sign. One who looks at them prisoned in a stained glass window feels unexplained sorrow.

In other frames are what appear to be swords. I think of them as purely ceremonial, for when my lord has me against the stone wall, one of his legs pressing between mine, I feel not the edge of his sword, though it hang at his side and sometime is thrust against me. True enough, I cannot argue that the force of his weight is not otherwhere!

One goes from frame to frame. I have been to the frame of the hammer, which is used to ring bells, and to the frame of the swan, where, at dawn, a bird rises out of the water and flies away on white wings, to show that cold is coming. I must provide for it. I have in mind a blue woolen cloak, to be trimmed in fur, and gloves.

Doll Boxes

The first, smiling one that squats over the rest
is the fattest and most saucer-eyed.
She's complacent.
But unscrew her, and see how this one's legs
are easier to find in the folds of the skirt,
and how the next one's forked.
Here's a waistband—
with each new layer she's getting less round.

Go on taking them apart. The floor's already littered with halves,
and they no longer have any suggestion of lushness.
I suppose you might as well look at the cruelly thin ones.

The man never does.
Sometimes he takes the outermost,
burrowing under her skirt in the dark,
parting her huge thighs with the flat of his hands,
and leaving soon after.
In his more tender moments he undresses her.
Softly he unscrews the tops of her heads
and lays each half neatly aside until he reaches the one he wants.

Which is that?
You know it'd be the one whose nipples stare straight at his chest
like two eggs on a platter!
As for the rest of the dolls, I'd say that the ones near the top layer
have accepted it. They sit by their front windows
and look out at the neighbors.
The others are starved, starved!
It's a shame, I tell you, but it can't be helped.
He can't fuck them all, can he?

Don't Say Love

Don't say 'love'—
We've said that already.
We've sighed "love," we've cried when
we've heard it in some old song.

Don't say 'love.' Say 'attachment,'
'infatuation,' 'passion for possession';
say 'ardor,' say 'rapture,' say
'capture of a partner's heart.'

Don't say 'love.' You won't get any closer.
Say, "Wanda! I must warn you! Shark attack!"
Say, "Calendulas, Clare?"
Say, "I'm rather bothered by her mother. Though I may be
oversensitive, it's true her dewlaps shudder when she laughs.
Still, the comfort of my Julia makes any small vexation
half."

Don't say 'love.' Burst into verb. Do.
Go on, muscle in. Come a cropper. Importune,
later this afternoon, some sumptuary for the hand of his heiress.
At least hack back the hydrangeas.
Don't sit around saying 'love.'

You say you're settled?
Refuse to move?
All right, then: be.
Be testy,
well dressed, be mossy-backed. Be positively
dalradian. Be useless, usually;
be his nemesis. Be a twin to the wind;
be beastly—don't say 'love.'

How to Swallow a Frog

Take the animal by one foot and swallow its head first.
It will then fold up like a parasol,
and the body will follow quite meekly.

I did not look into a mirror until the last green webs
had disappeared. The sight of a gaping mouth,
with small fans protruding, is not appetizing,
and brings thoughts of lost divers to mind.
It may cause the gorge to rise; it is not encouraged.
Simply persevere, and
do not watch yourself. This advice will serve you
all your life.

What I felt was the bones and the movement,
a painful hardness in the esophagus,
as if the small opening were stretched too wide.
But its muscles did their work,
moving the frog along like hands stuffing a sausage casing.
Think to yourself: if I must, I must.

The frog expanded in my stomach.
All the raised blisters on its back burst open from pressure,
and poison flowed out. I began to taste it in thin, oily saliva
at the sides of my tongue.

Then its small fingers grew longer and thinner, outdistancing
the webs until they reached into my veins. I believe
that if you cut into my arm at the elbow, it would dangle
from these live, green threads.

At night I think my skin is changing color, roughening.
My knees are turning outward, and not just for men. I long for
a stream, the sun's silver tunnels into its surface, the reeds' sway,
mud and the soft dark veils of the underwater leaves, the dragonflies,
the ceaseless working of the water boatmen, the trees wading
at the edge of the water and all the light and all the dark.

In the Dream of the Tiger

I had been given him.
Though my trees were very tall, they had no lower branches,
no green at eye level, and so, not much comfort.
They were only green clouds on tall poles.
But the tiger lurked in them and played high up,
letting his heavy dung fall past the window.
Wherever he walked he clawed holes.

I knew if it were not for the trees, the house would be surrounded
by soft yellow sea grass and orange flowers, blue white and yellow air.

II. The Betrayal of the Tiger

I betrayed him by not watching when I thought he might die.
When he fell from the tree I turned my back,
and stayed away from windows for the rest of the day.
I thought I could live with uneasy relief, and might have regarded him
like any other loss of possibility, but they said they saw him
running along the road by the ocean. Now the great truck
is following him.

III. The Responsibility for the Tiger

I've never wanted it, no.
What I want is hot water
for tea, for baths, for boil,
for soup, for wash.
There's a set of china I use for breakfast with a cup, saucer,
plate for toast, jam pot, chocolate pot, teapot, creamer, sugar bowl;
all on a tray lined with linen.
I want to think only of myself and to look out at the ocean.

IV. The Future of the Tiger

Where could he go? Could I take away his freedom
in order to have my own?
Let him pace the concrete,
the kids on shoulders shouting and staring,
the fake rocks, the peanut shells, the bars?

And yet why is he mine?

V. Why Adult Life is so Hard

You're the librarian. You keep track. You levy fines, you hunt up the
lost, you repair, always looking for the better tape, the kind that will
stick and be seen through. You answer questions, you deal with the
unappreciative, you keep, shelve, file, shush, straighten, repair, number,
lend. You learn the ends of stories.

VI. Is There Any Way Out?

Yes, but they all lead somewhere else.
A basketball outside is bouncing, bouncing,
slap,   slap,   slap,   slap,
against the concrete.

I intend to forget about the tiger.
I intend to become the tiger.

We Must Learn to Seem Empty

like the sand the world leaves its tracks on,
or the field where the battle was.
A short time afterwards, the sea has swept in,
the earth has licked blood from itself
and groomed the long grass risen from flattened places.
Already a bird sings, "didn't-see, didn't-see";
and a deer grazes, lured there by the promise of emptiness.
"You are the first," the field says, knowing
that beauty depends on an illusion of stillness.

Clouds on the surface of a great firemarked clay bowl
kept to hold water.
When the bowl is empty, it holds shadows.
In a house framed by leaves where lizards run the walls,
someone sings the right song for the evening.
Now the young men who play the bear
at the caged windows of girls feel less foolish,
the policeman at the corner near the cantina grows expansive.
Into the darkening sky goes the ball the children toss,
round like the night in the eye of a fish diving upward.

Let's live at the same speed as the things we watch!
We'll sit on the screened porch in steady moonlight,
feeling the chair beneath us, the things that stay.
We'll tell our stories,
aware that without the house and ourselves
there is only the dangerous, mosquito-ridden night.
We won't become empty, no matter how many times
we say 'death', or how many times
we smooth our faces to attract more life
and—not moving, not moving—
wait to see what replies.

Song Line through my House

You can of white shortening at the back of the shelf,
here is my attention. I sing your marriage with the flour
that lives in the canister sticky with fingerprints.
I see a journey during which you change form several times.
Do not fear melting.

I sing the half-forgotten: the small bottle of celery seed
opened twice, the snowball of a winter candle—all the things
unsettled when a drawer slides.

To the board games, their rules and instructions,
their play money, their plastic pieces,
to the papers by the telephone and their attempts at tyranny,
to the sheets and towels complacently folded, to the basket
of blocks and the toys in corners, I sing. I welcome you
out of background. This time I am looking.

I ask the dressers, whose smooth surfaces invite
invasion, the slippers on closet floors,
the smears on windows, the abandoned scooter,
the battered brown trash cans, to take the life
we have given along with our wear, and wake.

I make it my place to see what is
slumbering in the light.
I wish these unnoticed things
life after mine, and this is not a vain wish.
I've given away the shoes of the dead.

Edward Smallfield

Cattaraugus Creek

for Bill Jungels

Last August, wading the river's margin,
crossing those patches where water
rolls over shale, we headed
west, against the river, and maybe
we should have kept walking all winter.
Right now, in early March, our sneakers
would begin to thaw. We'd wonder
how we survived the worst months,
parked under the river ice like trout.
We'd wake again to our words, naming
trees and feelings as far as Omaha
and Salt Lake City. In April,
when the buds burst through tree bark,
we almost turn back. Sandblasted
by the wind our skin shines
like red brick and the mountains
hunch, dinosaurs who won't shift
their vast haunches, ignoring
our journey to the sea. That's where
we end up, two wizened old men, pale
and sexless, so small the viewer
can barely read us in the scroll.
The wind fills our mouths with cold
air, and under us the Pacific
shuffles its bitter chemistry.

Stain

My father sits in the kitchen, cleaning his rifle. The scent of gun oil reminds me of my childhood.

In the Paleolithic, I tell him, hunters preserved the bones of the animals they killed.

Under the pocket of his flannel shirt, so bright a man would see it through the leaves and not shoot, I notice a stain.

I don't know why my father wears that shirt tonight.

My father should be an old man, but he's younger than I am, in the prime of his life.

Nobody knows why they gathered those bones—I keep talking, though he doesn't seem to be listening—maybe to bring the animals to life again.

The subject, I tell him, is magic: that's where witches come from, and werewolves, from those stone age rituals.

Dark, untouched by gray, my father's hair is slicked back against his skull to conceal the density of the fibers, their furry quality.

I don't talk anymore. Instead I read: "Male and female witches met at night, generally in solitary places. Sometimes they flew, arriving on bride poles or broomsticks; sometimes they arrived on the backs of animals or transformed into animals themselves."

I remind him that the book has come to us from Italy, the country my mother's mother came from.

The stain must be blood, though I can't understand how my father could have gotten blood on his shirt. He used to hang back, at the edge of the circle, as if the skinning of the animal were a striptease he was ashamed to watch.

The rifle lies in pieces on the table, a kind of puzzle. My father reminds me of the army, of the need to know how to assemble the gun quickly, in the dark.

My father takes his shirt off. I don't want to look at his skin, so pale it seems somehow feminine.

My fever has turned itself inside out. I shiver, my teeth chatter, so my father has an excuse to wrap his shirt around my shoulders.

I must ask my father a question—something about those hunters, their desire to bring the animals to life again—but I can't say the words.

Firenze

for Kathleen

Gridlock in the Piazza
SS. Annunziata, rain
like cold spaghetti water
through a colander. At the hotel
Colleen folded her small body, snored
through her cold while we fumbled
together in bed, then dozed.
I want to reach back
for one moment, maybe
the view from the Duomo, light
seeping into us until we feel
alive inside a halo.
All I get is that first
afternoon, dingy rain, then
the next morning, patched
clouds and sun when I start
for the park with Colleen
and after a couple of hours
play we go back through the Via
della Colonna to the Accademia to look
at the slaves, those torsos caught
emerging from marble, my favorite
with his head still lost
entirely in stone.

Self Portrait with Thorn Necklace and Hummingbirds

Still wearing thorns and hummingbirds, Frida smiles at the party guests. Unaffected by her accident, she inhabits a supple body, lithe as a dancer's. To prove that she is unhurt, she raises her left leg until the foot is above her head.

Even without your field guide, you identify the hummingbirds in Frida's hair: ruby-throat, calliope, Lucifer's.

Frida compliments you on your shaved head. Something happens, she says, when a woman bares her skull.

All black, about the size of a sparrow, the hummingbird in the thorns of her necklace can't be identified, not even by you. Because the bird doesn't exist anywhere else, it has no name.

Frida can't keep her hands off your head. She strokes your bare scalp until a shadowy fuzz begins to show.

Plates of uneaten food. Lobsters, oysters, clams, crabs. Warm and flat, the champagne still tastes of rusty iron.

Where have the guests gone? Frida's jungle, the leaves she paints in the background, has begun to fill the room. You hear rain inside the foliage. Also music, a kind of broken carnival, a song played too slowly.

By now you are dancing with Frida, a lingering waltz. The ceiling and the walls have disappeared. Above you a few stars shine between the highest leaves. The rain continues, near enough to hear, but you aren't wet yet.

Sleepless Nights

for Eve

Somebody passes in the street under your window. That stranger walks to the corner, turns left from Cervantes onto Sargasso, then right on Soledad. Whoever it is hitchhikes south, disappears in Mexico.

The ceiling and the roof dissolve. You study the few stars visible through the eucalyptus over your house. Then the leaves fall, and the bare limbs deliver more stars. To pass the time, you invent new constellations.

Probably you don't think of any of these things, but of something I can't picture. A molecule the size of your fist, composed entirely of unnamed atoms. Far too many to count, but you count them anyway.

Somewhere between El Paso and San Luis Potosì, I've stopped the car. Maybe I need to pee, or just walk beside the road to stretch my legs. Because the heater in the Volkswagen is broken, you and your mother sleep huddled in sleeping bags. The desert hangs from an enormous moon. The sand I walk on glows, a luminous substance, radioactive. I could drive anywhere, in any direction, if I knew where to go.

When you tell me you can't sleep, I think of that night in the desert. As if my confusion could be a lesson, something you might learn from.

Lying on your back in the bottom of the boat, you feel the river unravel. Steeped in high leaves, the light seeps into your skin. You drift for miles, still wide awake.

Open Windows

House finches and towhees, warblers
with yellow butts—when I borrow
the binoculars I don't see

what you see. I can't
fix a name to those rusty
throats, don't even

bother to focus—leaves
stain the sun, a green
smudge, too fluid to hold.

•

A few notes
seep through—
awkward as a child
who studies too
hard, licks her pencil
before she answers. Not
a child—a woman
in her fifties who plays
the piece as if it might
break. Then begins
again, faster,
somebody who runs
to catch a train.

•

Dark as the acacia
against the stars the cat

separates from the night,
bits of iron stroked by a magnet.

•

The neighbor's dog paces the darkness. His chain rattles, and he whimpers softly as he walks. He wants to be a good dog, knows he isn't supposed to bark, but he can't help himself when he smells a raccoon or possum moving through the weeds at the back of the yard. Kathy comes to the door, tells him to hush. He's quiet, then barks again, wildly, when the scent finds him.

●

After summer, early nights.
Walls the color of ripe pears.

●

Green on the bird's
back marks it
as Anna's
Hummingbird sixty
beats per
second it hovers
head dips beak
probes the mute
buds for more
sugar to feed
this engine
throbbing blossom
to blossom
where it finds
more throbbing

Insomnia

Pick up the dictionary. Note the ink's carbony scent, insistent in the darkness. Touch the words, though you can't see them, arrayed in strict sequence like passengers in their seats on a train. And when the train enters a tunnel, the air in the car darkens, thick as the night inside your room. The jolt that stops them is quiet, no clatter, just the abrupt absence of motion. Then silence. These are polite passengers. Here and there a noise of paper shuffling, as some pretend to read the books and magazines they can no longer see. Time passes. Sobbing, the sound of shoes on the carpeted floor, the door at the back of the car. Perhaps they escape, flow into the tunnel and then the bright sunshine above the Apennines. A woman turns to the man beside her. Except for them, the train is entirely empty. She does not ask his name. When he takes her hand, her nails print their shapes in the flesh of his palm. This is just practice, she says. We live in an age of industrial decline, and we'll learn to sit quietly in the growing cold. Pick up the dictionary, he answers. Forget the words, since it's too late for them. Notice the letters, especially the first one. You'll only need the first one. See how the monk has fashioned the letter from a serpent contrived of innumerable golden scales. Each gold ounce shines, a tiny sun. Count, though you can't, those countless coins. Keep counting as your eyes dim. Sleep.

Labor Day

A pop
fly hangs, white
speck against a sky
pearly with moisture: last
of the ninth, bases
loaded, two
out—the runners
go, are going, have
gone. Waiting
for the ball
to come down I pound
the glove till my fist
smells of leather
and oil. At the union
picnic the Senator
shakes the last
hand and the last
little flag is lost
in high grass. Already
winter begins and snow
fills the air with white
flecks falling all over
me and the girls
on the bases are married
and divorced, the farm's
sold and the white
pines are cut
down by the new
owner and I move
to California, divorced
and married again I pound
the glove till my fist
smells of leather
and oil, waiting
for the ball, a pop
fly

Portrait of Colleen as the Goddess Flora

Late Renaissance, because the painter flaunts
his knowledge of anatomy. Small muscles

tense as the girl extends her arm
into the sun. Noon

brightens the right side of her face
while shadow envelopes the whole

left of her body. No forced tension
distorts her pose. She steps

forward, toward you. Her lips
part slightly, as if she might speak.

A child, about six years old.
In her hand the blossoms tremble.

On them the painter has lavished
all of his skill. The petals

glow, suffused with sun.
A few buds shrivel,

ready to crumble,
like ash, at your touch.

You look at the girl's face again.
Her eyes, wide open, watch you

as she wonders
if you'll reach

for the flowers
she thrusts toward your hand.

Black Dog

I seldom notice that shelf
anymore with the eight low-fired black
clay animals from Oaxaca, whistles
with slits in their bases. We bought all eight
at the same shop about two blocks
from the *mercado* and when I dropped
your favorite one, catching
the fragile toy just inches from the floor,
the old woman behind the counter laughed
and I realized that we were paying
less than a buck for the whole batch.
Still, I would hate to lose one now,
even the duplicate rooster, certainly
not the dog I almost broke, hunkered
on his hind legs, front paws held up
as if he expected me to save him.

Prostate

An eel in a Swedish poem: "white, frighteningly big, blind, coiling in and out of the riddles of its body..." That's a fairly accurate picture of the gland I imagine.

A secret. At work inside the body. A woman in an attic who writes, then locks the pages in a drawer.

A worker whose business is pleasure. The manufacture of desire.

Stroked by sound, the prostate shines. A song, the notes too high to hear, projects shadows on a screen. The center of attention, a star irradiated by flashbulbs.

I lie with my face to the wall. A boy who pretends to sleep, so his parents won't know that he hears what is happening.

"Hey, Dr. Vendler," the woman who takes the picture yells into the hallway, "you wanna look at a prostate?"

"A partly muscular gland at the base of the bladder and surrounding the urethra in male mammals, providing some of the chemicals necessary for the production of sperm."

As a man grows older the prostate stiffens. Loses elasticity. Enlarges. Presses the bladder, creates a boyish urge to pee constantly. Becomes cancerous, spreads throughout the body.

A metaphor for desire. What we use, what we don't use. What uses us.

The doctor and nurse study the pictures. The star revealed in her many poses. Lateral, dorsal, transverse. Prostrate. So bare the glare hurts. Not naked, but stripped, peeled.

Written in secret. Locked in a drawer. The urge to speak what isn't spoken.

The Garden of Earthly Delights

In our world the odors feed us. Scents of ripe strawberries and salt water pervade the space between the varnish and the canvas where we live. Our pores absorb the atmosphere. That's why we're naked. We breathe through our skins like frogs.

The first panel: a newborn planet, innocent as a lizard with three heads...

A scholar explains our world as an alphabet of symbols, easy to read with a key he possesses. His breath against the varnish smells of wine and eels.

Ravens stroke the air. Their wings define the sky's body. Their bodies, black as letters, spell desire.

The scholar continues his lecture: pig = false priest, sex; fruit = adultery, sex; rat = lies against church, sex; fish = false prophet, sex; flame = hell fire, sex; breast = fertility, sex; mussel shell = adultery, sex...

Disguised as a unicorn, Charles Darwin drinks from a stream. Beside him a wildebeest peers through Sigmund Freud's suspicious eyes.

In the middle panel a ripe world shines. Here we pursue the pleasures of maturity: we ride pigs around a salty pool, bury our heads in blackberries. Why don't they fuck? someone asks in your world, where questions are still possible.

Have you noticed our skins? White as ice cream, firm as peaches plucked too early...

Another scholar. No codes here, no keys. We're an assault, an effort to call a final judgement down, force a return to Eden. According to this expert, we witnessed, as an altarpiece, the Adamite orgies. He describes the scene so precisely that you can smell the sweat of the participants, taste their secretions.

Strawberries the size of basketballs. An owl big enough to embrace.

Some nights we disengage ourselves from the canvas, slip under the varnish to arrange ourselves in new postures. Combinations less inventive but more comfortable than the positions the painter has chosen for us. In the morning, when the museum opens, the landscape looks the same, but some of us have switched places.

Beside the unicorn and the wildebeest a water buffalo grazes with an air of youthful innocence reminiscent of Einstein in the patent office.

Houses flare in the last panel, bright against the night sky. Intimate fires. The flames know what the wood wants. With his tongue a demon explores a song engraved on a pair of rosy buttocks. A night of games and knives...

Sometimes we gaze through the varnish into your world of decay and death. Clothing robs your bodies of expression. Your stiff faces, masks of a fierce civility, terrify us. You can't see our world. Your own preoccupations shine back at you.

An alphabet, a scholar says, of desires.

The varnish sweats in this climate. Time erodes our shell. We watch the membrane that protects us scraped away by auto exhaust, the breath of visitors and our guards. Shall we writhe and cry? Beg a scholar to restore us, apply fresh varnish in an airless room? We wait to shrivel in real light...

Blood

After midnight my uncles skin the season's last buck. A small deer, maybe a hundred pounds, gutted, his slender antlers barely legal.

From our attic we can see everything. Blood in puddles, the glint of knives. Because we've seen so much, we believe nothing, certainly not these old men, too feeble to peel the dead animal.

My grandfather, who's been dead for twenty-five years, drags his thumbnail across the deer's belly, from the base of the throat all the way to the balls. Then he jerks the skin away in one piece, tosses the bloody hide in a corner.

I remind you of my uncles' names, though by now they look so much alike that I can't tell them apart. You say that you want to steal the deer's hide, wrap the bloody fur around your skin and dance.

My father hovers at the light's edge. Younger than the others, up past his bedtime, he rubs his eyes. If you ask him about this tomorrow, he'll tell you he was somewhere else.

The old men relax on the garage floor. Most sit cross-legged. A few squat. One lies on his back, oblivious to the cold concrete.

When you ask me what the old men say, I don't bother to read their lips. I've heard the stories so often that I recite them in my sleep.

The deer has been disassembled. Scattered on the garage floor, the pieces remind us of a clock dissected by a child. You recall your anatomy textbook, name the lungs and heart for me, the gall bladder, kidneys, and spleen.

A bottle passes. Cigarettes are smoked and snuffed. The old men sleep.

Just look away, you tell me, and the whole scene disappears. I close my eyes, and the world shrinks to the size of my body. I feel your breath against my face, wet patches where our bodies touch.

An odor hangs in the air. That's blood, you tell me, a memory of the deer. We agree that the smell reminds us of seawater. Maybe, I say, the scent belongs to us, a residue of the chemistry of your skin against mine.

How the Late October Novel Begins

The scent of the forest floor, mushroom and pine and decay—that's how the dream ends, after the woman's body stops squirming, whether in pleasure or pain he can't tell. As he lies in bed, half-awake, the dream fades, and the smell of death in the house assaults him. You haven't decided yet whose death should obsess him. Probably you'll choose his father, though that seems somehow wrong, a deflection of your mother's death when you were about the character's age. Perhaps your whole approach is too oblique. Even the title has been stolen, but also incorrectly translated, misremembered. At least the young man's teacher is clear in your mind. A heavy woman, fleshy and pale, she flushes when she lectures. While she speaks the class ignores her. Only your character listens, and he can't understand what she means. She lectures on the brain, so that you'll have to buy a biology book, learn the names of the lobes, what each one does. Today she digresses, as she so often does, and discusses the alchemy of scents. Of course she fascinates the young man. He wants to tell her about the smell of death in his house, the scent of the forest floor in his dreams. You'll have to repeat the dreams, creating a kind of counterpoint, gradually revealing their content. You must hint at a subtext inside him, a dark inner life that he doesn't understand. You must also work in the crimes, a series of rapes and murders that haunt the inhabitants of the town. Your protagonist feels linked to those crimes by his dreams, but he can't admit that to himself. Of course you won't provide all the details—you don't want to write pulp fiction—but you must hint at sinister particulars you won't reveal until later, if at all. Will you allow the reader to believe that the young man may be implicated in those crimes, not just in his own mind, but in reality as well? You remember the fragment whose title you've stolen, how the boat's motor throbs at the center of the prose, a metaphor so insistent that your head aches as you read. Maybe you should have begun as that other author did, or maybe you shouldn't have begun at all. You try to imagine the young man in his bed as he wakes from the dream you find so disturbing. But he insists on standing at his teacher's desk, after her lecture, waiting to speak to her. Her perfume, mingled with the scent of her body, reminds him of something.

Running

for Eve

Out there, in the deep grass, wildflowers flare
on their wiry stems. I wish I knew their names,
common and Latin. Then I could bore you
properly, then I could chant pure information,
stuff you don't want to hear, but will care about,
when you're my age, and have forgotten
everything. Keep running. If I don't
keep running, I tell myself, I'll petrify,
become a man in a story who ends up
pointing to where the old road used to be.
So we move together through this dust,
through the weedy California August. Let me catch
my breath, if you let me breathe we can run
forever, if you want, past the fence
into the grass, stopping now and then
to pick the stickers from our socks.
After the hills give up and lie flat
the grass around us won't be grass,
but a cash crop, maybe alfalfa, thick
and green, the odor intoxicating,
as we move more slowly, pausing
to drink from garden hoses
behind farm houses in the valley.
Then we can hitch a ride across
the Sierras and western Nevada, halfway
to the salt flats. I can tell you
Wyoming and Nebraska, Highway 80
just as direct and bleak as it was
when I drove west, not east, when you
were two and I was still married
to your mother. Maybe in upstate
New York we can stop in front
of a hospital and stare at the lights

of the maternity ward as I used to
fifteen years ago and at the Atlantic
edge we'll head south toward Tierra
del Fuego or maybe we'll just keep walking
across the waves. Right now, though, nails
and gravel rattle in my left knee and you
have geometry homework due tomorrow
and a basketball game on Saturday.
So we turn at the gate, limping back
along the same dusty track, abandoning
this language that isn't
our bodies breathing hard right here
where you are the one
who must keep running
long after I'm through.

February

for my mother

Each year as I grow older I think less often about dying.

Sometimes I even pass the anniversary of your death without thinking of you. I immerse myself in the details of my present life, and I'm excused from visiting the house on Walnut Street again. Not the real house, inhabited now by a family of strangers, but the other house, where the smell of the oil furnace still persists. That smell, and the thick fog—two of the many things I noticed for the first time that winter. Even my body was new, someone I couldn't trust, especially when I'd find myself in the middle of a slow dance with my erection boring into a girl's thigh.

Your death connected itself with my growing up, almost as if you had chosen to die so I could grow up. Death and life were separated by a membrane. Some things passed through while others didn't. The dead couldn't communicate with the living, but the fact of death carried a message I wanted to decode. In bed with a woman for the first time, on a mattress so small that one of us always had to be on top of the other, I heard a voice outside in the street that reminded me of you.

That voice didn't sound like yours, but the moments were linked by their persistence, scraps I wanted to keep until I could fit everything together. Now that I'm older than you were when you died, older than you can ever be, I want to tell you that there are no pieces and no puzzle, nothing to hold on to or store up, only things passing and already gone, but you can't hear or understand, you're too young.

August

Tonight the homeless guy on the corner mumbles
something about a sky full of angels.

Under the streetlight
the magnolia's fleshy petals glow
white, almost transparent,
their slow explosion halfway spent.

In the movie the boy hides from the Nazis
as a Nazi. He slides the skin
near the tip of his penis
forward, ties a string around it
to fake a foreskin.

Quiet streets, the car an envelope.
We talk about cruelty, decide we know
nothing. While we speak
Mozart fills the air
with joyful noise.

Tomorrow you'll drive back to school,
open a book full of equations
and listen as the Pacific stutters
its severe arithmetic, nothing
about fathers and daughters
drifting apart.

For a few more minutes
we talk quietly in the car
outside your mother's house.

Somewhere nearby a young thief
slips through an attic window,
finds the whole house under him
open, dark, and vulnerable.

Secret Lives

An author writes of his father's life. In a vast house the old man inhabits a single room. Each day he chooses the same suit from his full closets. He seems a photograph of himself, unchanging as his business crumbles around him. Younger women appear with him in snapshots. After the old man's heart attack, the son discovers a supply of condoms. I abandon the book, still open, on a table in the library.

At dinner with a couple I don't know, friends of my wife, I hear a curious story. The man, about my age, explains that his father led a double life. Two wives, two sets of children. He speaks of his recent efforts, long after his father's death, to locate the members of that other family. When he found a half-sister, he couldn't understand her reluctance to meet with him. She was dying of cancer. What, he asks, could she have had to lose? Finally she agreed to see him. The man does not describe that meeting. As he speaks it becomes clear that he was a member of his father's second family, a character in his father's secret life.

That night I can't sleep. I remember my father's hands, so big that his coffee cup always seemed about to break. In spite of his strength, my father remains insubstantial. Sometimes I wonder if he hired an actor to portray him. Especially after my mother died, when I felt that his real life must be elsewhere. With his friends at work, or with a woman he had to keep secret for some reason I couldn't understand. An actor's most difficult role must be to establish his character on an empty stage. Light seeps through the curtains, a stain on the darkness in which I've failed to sleep. I can't bear the thought that my father may have had no secret life.

February 14, 1994

So much marsh, you can't see
where it ends—that's what
I'd give you, the light
a little patchy, smudged by mist
as if somebody wants to erase
all this, and fails, while the birds
rise—herons, egrets, grebes—
yes, I've learned the names
from you, but not the shapes,
to me those shadows are just
shadows, stringy meat
that must taste of clams
and the oil our tankers spill,
and just for the pleasure
of hearing I ask for more names—
loons, buffleheads, mergansers—
and as you speak I see
you sweat in the winter sun
after so much walking, your wet
skin shares the chemistry
of this marsh, iodine and salt,
as if the water were our bodies
turned inside out, and you look
west, toward the Farallones,
where giant sponges swell
on nuclear waste—
avocet, you say, widgeon, coot,
godwit, bittern, stilt, plover—
I wonder when you'll come
to the end and if
you'll begin again,
though by now the sun
sits on the water
and in that glare you can't see
where it ends, this marsh
I'd give you, if the water
wasn't here already, and you
inside its salty light.

Toni Mirosevich has had work appear in *The Kenyon Review*, *ZYZZYVA*, *The Seattle Review* and various other journals. While receiving an MFA in Creative Writing at San Francisco State she won the Academy of American Poets Award, The Anne Fields Poetry Prize, *The Americas Review* Poetry Prize and most recently was awarded first place in the 1994 *San Francisco Bay Guardian* Poetry Contest. She teaches creative writing at San Francisco State and Santa Clara Universities and lives in Pacifica with her girlfriend and numerous animals.

Charlotte Muse is the author of *The Comfort Teacher*, a chapbook published by Heyeck Press. Her work has also been published in the anthology *Coastlight*, and in various journals and small magazines. She is co-host of the poetry radio show, "Out of Our Minds," on KKUP-FM, Cupertino. She has taught Poetry Writing at San Francisco State University, where she is completing her MFA in Creative Writing, and is currently teaching Writing and Appreciating Poetry at U. C. Berkeley Extension. She has been Book Editor for the *Palo Alto Weekly* newspaper, and has written reviews and articles for that paper and for the *Peninsula Times-Tribune*, the *San Jose Mercury News*, the *San Francisco Chronicle*, and the *San Francisco Review of Books*. She has been a voting member of the Bay Area Book Reviewers' Association, and an active participant in the Bay Area Book Awards. She has two children and sometimes dreams of a less complicated life.

Edward Smallfield has taught creative writing at San Francisco State University and now teaches a poetry workshop through University of California at Berkeley Extension. His poems have appeared in *Caliban*, *Ironwood*, *Manoa*, *Painted Hills Review*, *ZYZZYVA*, and other periodicals. He lives with his wife and daughter in Albany, California.